The Nigh Before My Birthday

GROSSET & DUNLAP

Published by the Penguin Group

Penguin Group (USA), 375 Hudson Street, New York, New York 10014, USA

USA | Canada | UK | Ireland | Australia | New Zealand | India | South Africa | China

Penguin Books Ltd, Registered Offices: 80 Strand, London WC2R 0RL, England

For more information about the Penguin Group visit penguin.com

Text copyright © 2014 by Natasha Wing. Illustrations copyright © 2014 by Penguin Group (USA). All rights reserved. Published by Grosset & Dunlap, a division of Penguin Young Readers Group, 345 Hudson Street, New York, New York 10014. GROSSET & DUNLAP is a registered trademark of Penguin Group (USA). Printed in the U.S.A.

Library of Congress Cataloging-in-Publication Data is available.

ISBN 978-0-448-48000-8   10 9 8 7

ALWAYS LEARNING   PEARSON

The Night Before My Birthday

By Natasha Wing
Illustrated by Amy Wummer

Grosset & Dunlap
An Imprint of Penguin Group (USA)

'Twas the night before my birthday.
Hooray! It's almost here!

It may not be a holiday,
but it's the best day of the year.

The invites were out. The streamers were strung.
The presents were wrapped. The banner was hung.

I blew up some balloons.
I like the ones with stars best.
"Time for bed now," said Mom.
"We'll blow up the rest."

So I put on my jammies,
which felt a bit tight.
Tomorrow Mom will measure
and record my new height.

That night I nestled all
snug in my bed,
while visions of birthday
gifts danced in my head.

In the morning I woke
from a deep, sleepy slumber.
Yay! Today is the day
I turn a new number!

"Congratulations!" said Mom.
"You're a year older."
"This year I'll grow taller
and run faster!" I told her.

Just an hour till the party.
It was sure hard to wait.
Mom and Dad set the table
with party napkins and plates.

There were fun hats and toot horns,
and for each guest, party favors.

Dad took out cartons of ice cream
in three different flavors.

Everything was ready.
What could go wrong?
Soon I'd be hearing
the "happy birthday" song.

Then out in the kitchen
there arose such a clatter.
We ran down the hallway
to see what was the matter.

Balloons went *Pop! Pop!*
Mom let out a scream.
Our kitty was lapping up
melted ice cream!

Mom checked in the freezer.
"We don't have any more."

"Come on, birthday kid," said Dad.
"Let's go to the store."

Away to the market,
we made a mad dash,

grabbed cartons of ice cream,
and checked out in a flash.

"We're home!" Dad called as we came into the house. Yet the place seemed empty— it was as quiet as a mouse.

When what to my wondering eyes should appear,
but a room full of friends shouting,
"Surprise! We're already here!"

The gifts—oh, so many!
The cards—how funny!
I got books and games
and, from Grandma, some money!

Then out went the lights,
and in came the cake.
I puffed out my cheeks.
What wish should I make?

Everyone gathered around and—on the count of three—

sang at the top of their lungs, "Happy birthday!"—to me!

Now it's time to draw
your new age on the cake.
When you blow out *your* candles,
what wish will you make?